THE OLD PEABODY PEW :
A CHRISTMAS ROMANCE
OF A COUNTRY CHURCH

By
KATE DOUGLAS WIGGIN

Double 9
BOOKS

The Old Peabody Pew : A Christmas Romance of a Country Church

by **Kate Douglas Wiggin**

ISBN: 978-93-57274-92-0

Published by

DOUBLE 9 BOOKS

2/13-B, Ansari Road, Daryaganj,
New Delhi – 110002
info@double9books.com
www.double9books.com
Tel. 011-40042856

ABOUT THE AUTHOR

Kate Douglas Wiggin was an American educator, author, and composer who lived from September 28, 1856, until August 24, 1923. She also created collections of children's songs in addition to writing children's books, most famously the classic Rebecca of Sunnybrook Farm. In San Francisco, she established the city's first free kindergarten in 1878. (the Silver Street Free Kindergarten). She also started a kindergarten teacher training program in the 1880s with her sister. In an era when kids were often seen as cheap labor, Kate Wiggin dedicated her whole life to the welfare of kids. Wiggin traveled to California to research kindergarten instruction. She started teaching in San Francisco with the help of her sister Nora, and the two were crucial in establishing more than 60 kindergartens for the underprivileged in Oakland and San Francisco. She relocated from California to New York, and because she was out of kindergarten assignments, she focused on literature. Her submissions of The Story of Patsy and The Bird's Christmas Carol were immediately accepted by Houghton, Mifflin & Co. She had storytelling ability in addition to being a good singer, guitarist, and composer of settings for her poems. She was a skilled orator as well.

CONTENTS

Dedication

To a certain handful of dear New England women of names unknown to the world, dwelling in a certain quiet village, alike unknown:—

We have worked together to make our little corner of the great universe a pleasanter place in which to live, and so we know, not only one another's names, but something of one another's joys and sorrows, cares and burdens, economies, hopes, and anxieties.

We all remember the dusty uphill road that leads to the green church common. We remember the white spire pointing upward against a background of blue sky and feathery elms. We remember the sound of the bell that falls on the Sabbath morning stillness, calling us across the daisy-sprinkled meadows of June, the golden hayfields of July, or the dazzling whiteness and deep snowdrifts of December days. The little cabinet-organ that plays the doxology, the hymn-books from which we sing "Praise God from whom all blessings flow," the sweet freshness of the old meeting-house, within and without—how we have toiled to secure and preserve these humble mercies for ourselves and our children!

There really *is* a Dorcas Society, as you and I well know, and one not unlike that in these pages; and you and I have lived through many discouraging, laughable, and beautiful experiences while we emulated the Bible Dorcas, that woman "full of good works and alms deeds."

There never was a Peabody Pew in the Tory Hill Meeting-House, and Nancy's love story and Justin's never happened within its century-old walls; but I have imagined only one of the many romances that have had their birth under the shadow of that steeple, did we but realize it.

As you have sat there on open-windowed Sundays, looking across purple clover-fields to blue distant mountains, watching the palm-leaf fans swaying to and fro in the warm stillness before sermon time, did not the place seem full of memories, for has not the life of two villages ebbed and flowed beneath that ancient roof? You heard the hum of droning bees and followed the airy wings of butterflies fluttering over the gravestones in the old churchyard, and underneath almost every moss-grown tablet some humble romance lies buried and all but forgotten.

If it had not been for you, I should never have written this story, so I give it back to you tied with a sprig from Ophelia's nosegay; a spring of "rosemary, that's for remembrance."

K. D. W.

August, 1907

CHAPTER I

E dgewood, like all the other villages along the banks of the Saco, is full of sunny slopes and leafy hollows. There are little, rounded, green-clad hillocks that might, like their scriptural sisters, "skip with joy," and there are grand, rocky hills tufted with gaunt pine trees—these leading the eye to the splendid heights of a neighbour State, where snow-crowned peaks tower in the blue distance, sweeping the horizon in a long line of majesty.

Tory Hill holds its own among the others for peaceful beauty and fair prospect, and on its broad, level summit sits the white-painted Orthodox Meeting-House. This faces a grassy common where six roads meet, as if the early settlers had determined that no one should lack salvation because of a difficulty in reaching its visible source.

The old church has had a dignified and fruitful past, dating from that day in 1761 when young Paul Coffin received his call to preach at a stipend of fifty pounds sterling a year; answering "that never having heard of any Uneasiness among the people about his Doctrine or manner of life, he declared himself pleased to Settle as Soon as might be Judged Convenient."

But that was a hundred and fifty years ago, and much has happened since those simple, strenuous old days. The chastening hand of time has been laid somewhat heavily on the town as well as on the church. Some of her sons have marched to the wars and died on the field of honour; some, seeking better fortunes, have gone westward; others, wearying of village life, the rocky soil, and rigours of farm-work, have become entangled in the noise and competition, the rush and strife, of cities. When the sexton rings the bell nowadays, on a Sunday morning, it seems to have lost some of its old-time militant strength, something of its hope and courage; but it still rings, and although the Davids and Solomons, the Matthews, Marks, and Pauls of former congregations have left few descendants to perpetuate their labours, it will go on ringing as long as there is a Tabitha, a Dorcas, a Lois, or a Eunice left in the community.

This sentiment had been maintained for a quarter of a century, but it was now especially strong, as the old Tory Hill Meeting-House had been undergoing for several years more or less extensive repairs. In point of fact, the still stronger word, "improvements," might be used with impunity; though whenever the Dorcas Society, being female, and therefore possessed of notions regarding comfort and beauty, suggested any serious changes, the finance committees, which were inevitably male in their composition, generally disapproved of making any impious alterations in a tabernacle, chapel, temple, or any other building used for purposes of worship. The majority in these august bodies asserted that their ancestors had prayed and sung there for a century and a quarter, and what was good enough for their ancestors was entirely suitable for them. Besides, the community was becoming less and less prosperous, and church-going was growing more and more lamentably uncommon, so that even from a business standpoint, any sums expended upon decoration by a poor and struggling parish would be worse than wasted.

In the particular year under discussion in this story, the valiant and progressive Mrs. Jeremiah Burbank was the president of the Dorcas Society, and she remarked privately and publicly that if her ancestors liked a smoky church, they had a perfect right to the enjoyment of it, but that she didn't intend to sit through meeting on winter Sundays, with her white ostrich feather turning grey and her eyes smarting and watering, for the rest of her natural life.

Whereupon, this being in a business session, she then and there proposed to her already hypnotized constituents ways of earning enough money to build a new chimney on the other side of the church.

An awe-stricken community witnessed this beneficent act of vandalism, and, finding that no thunderbolts of retribution descended from the skies, greatly relished the change. If one or two aged persons complained that they could not sleep as sweetly during sermon-time in the now clear atmosphere of the church, and that the parson's eye was keener than before, why, that was a mere detail, and could not be avoided; what was the loss of a little sleep compared with the discoloration of Mrs. Jere Burbank's white ostrich feather and the smarting of Mrs. Jere Burbank's eyes?

A new furnace followed the new chimney, in due course, and as a sense of comfort grew, there was opportunity to notice the lack of beauty. Twice in sixty years had some well-to-do summer parishioner painted the interior of the church at his own expense; but although the roof had been many times reshingled, it had always persisted in leaking, so that the ceiling and walls were disfigured by unsightly spots and stains and streaks. The question of shingling was tacitly felt to be outside the feminine domain, but as there were five women to one man in the church membership, the feminine domain was frequently obliged to extend its limits into the hitherto unknown. Matters of tarring and water-proofing were discussed in and out of season, and the very school-children imbibed knowledge concerning lapping, overlapping, and cross-lapping, and first and second quality of cedar shingles. Miss Lobelia Brewster, who had a rooted distrust of anything done by mere man, created strife by remarking that she could have stopped the leak in the belfry tower with her red flannel petticoat better than the Milltown man with his new-fangled rubber sheeting, and that the last shingling could have been more thoroughly done by a "female infant babe"; whereupon the person criticized retorted that he wished Miss Lobelia Brewster had a few infant babes to "put on the job—he'd like to see 'em try." Meantime several male members of the congregation, who at one time or another had sat on the roof during the hottest of the dog days to see that shingling operations we're conscientiously and skilfully performed, were very pessimistic as to any satisfactory result ever being achieved.

"The angle of the roof—what they call the 'pitch'—they say that that's always been wrong," announced the secretary of the Dorcas in a business session.

"Is it that kind of pitch that the Bible says you can't touch without being defiled? If not, I vote that we unshingle the roof and alter the pitch!" This proposal came from a sister named Maria Sharp, who had valiantly offered the year before to move the smoky chimney with her own hands, if the "men-folks" wouldn't.

But though the incendiary suggestion of altering the pitch was received with applause at the moment, subsequent study of the situation proved that such a proceeding was entirely beyond the modest means of the society. Then there arose an ingenious and militant carpenter in a neighbouring village, who asserted that he would shingle the meeting-house roof for such and such a sum, and agree to drink every drop of water that would leak in afterward. This was felt by all parties to be a promise attended by extraordinary risks, but it was accepted nevertheless, Miss Lobelia Brewster remarking that the rash carpenter, being already married, could not marry a Dorcas anyway, and even if he died, he was not a resident of Edgewood, and therefore could be more easily spared, and that it would be rather exciting, just for a change, to see a man drink himself to death with rain-water. The expected tragedy never occurred, however, and the inspired shingler fulfilled his promise to the letter, so that before many months the Dorcas Society proceeded, with incredible exertion, to earn more money, and the interior of the church was neatly painted and made as fresh as a rose. With no smoke, no rain, no snow nor melting ice to defile it, the good old landmark that had been pointing its finger Heavenward for over a century would now be clean and fragrant for years to come, and the weary sisters leaned back in their respective rocking-chairs and drew deep breaths of satisfaction.

These breaths continued to be drawn throughout an unusually arduous haying season; until, in fact, a visitor from a neighbouring city was heard to remark that the Tory Hill Meeting-House would be one of the best preserved and pleasantest churches in the whole State of Maine, if only it were suitably carpeted.

This thought had secretly occurred to many a Dorcas in her hours of pie-making, preserving, or cradle-rocking, but had been promptly extinguished as flagrantly extravagant and altogether impossible. Now that it had been openly mentioned, the contagion of the idea spread, and in a month every sort of honest machinery for the increase of funds had been set in motion: harvest suppers, pie sociables, old folk's concerts, apron sales, and, as a last resort, a subscription paper, for the church floor measured hundreds of square yards, and the carpet committee announce that a good ingrain could not be purchased, even with the church discount, for less than ninety-seven cents a yard.

The Dorcases took out their pencils, and when they multiplied the surface of the floor by the price of the carpet per yard, each Dorcas attaining a result entirely different from all the others, there was a shriek of dismay, especially from the secretary, who had included in her mathematical operation certain figures in her possession representing the cubical contents of the church and the offending pitch of the roof, thereby obtaining a product that would have dismayed a Croesus. Time sped and efforts increased, but the Dorcases were at length obliged to clip the wings of their desire and content themselves with carpeting the pulpit and pulpit steps, the choir, and the two aisles, leaving the floor in the pews until some future year.

How the women cut and contrived and matched that hardly-bought red ingrain carpet, in the short December afternoons that ensued after its purchase; so that, having failed to be ready for Thanksgiving, it could be finished for the Christmas festivities!

They were sewing in the church, and as the last stitches were being taken, Maria Sharp suddenly ejaculated in her impulsive fashion:—

"Wouldn't it have been just perfect if we could have had the pews repainted before we laid the new carpet!"

"It would, indeed," the president answered; "but it will take us all winter to pay for the present improvements, without any thought of fresh paint. If only we had a few more men-folks to help along!"

"Or else none at all!" was Lobelia Brewster's suggestion. "It's havin' so few that keeps us all stirred up. If there wa'n't any anywheres, we'd have women deacons and carpenters and painters, and get along first rate; for somehow the supply o' women always holds out, same as it does with caterpillars an' flies an' grasshoppers!"

Everybody laughed, although Maria Sharp asserted that she for one was not willing to be called a caterpillar simply because there were too many women in the universe.

"I never noticed before how shabby and scarred and dirty the pews are," said the minister's wife as she looked at them reflectively.

"I've been thinking all the afternoon of the story about the poor old woman and the lily," and Nancy Wentworth's clear voice broke into the discussion. "Do you remember some one gave her a stalk of Easter lilies and she set them in a glass pitcher on the kitchen table? After looking at them for a few minutes, she got up from her chair and washed the pitcher until the glass shone. Sitting down again, she glanced at the little window. It would never do; she had forgotten how dusty and blurred it was, and she took her cloth and burnished the panes. Then she scoured the table, then the floor, then blackened the stove before she sat down to her knitting. And of course the lily had done it all, just by showing, in its whiteness, how grimy everything else was."

The minister's wife who had been in Edgewood only a few months, looked admiringly at Nancy's bright face, wondering that five-and-thirty years of life, including ten of school-teaching, had done so little to mar its serenity. "The lily story is as true as the gospel!" she exclaimed, "and I can see how one thing has led you to another in making the church comfortable. But my husband says that two coats of paint on the pews would cost a considerable sum."

"How about cleaning them? I don't believe they've had a good hard washing since the flood." The suggestion came from Deacon Miller's wife to the president.

"They can't even be scrubbed for less than fifteen or twenty dollars, for I thought of that and asked Mrs. Simpson yesterday, and she said twenty cents a pew was the cheapest she could do it for."

"We've done everything else," said Nancy Wentworth, with a twitch of her thread; "why don't we scrub the pews? There's nothing in the orthodox creed to forbid, is there?"

"Speakin' o' creeds," and here old Mrs. Sargent paused in her work, "Elder Ransom from Acreville stopped with us last night, an' he tells me they recite the Euthanasian Creed every few Sundays in the Episcopal Church. I didn't want him to know how ignorant I was, but I looked up the word in the dictionary. It means easy death, and I can't see any sense in that, though it's a terrible long creed, the Elder says, an' if it's any longer 'n ourn, I should think anybody *might* easy die learnin' it!"

"I think the word is Athanasian," ventured the minister's wife.

"Elder Ransom's always plumb full o' doctrine," asserted Miss Brewster, pursuing the subject. "For my part, I'm glad he preferred Acreville to our place. He was so busy bein' a minister, he never got round to bein' a human creeter. When he used to come to sociables and picnics, always lookin' kind o' like the potato blight, I used to think how complete he'd be if he had a foldin' pulpit under his coat tails; they make foldin' beds nowadays, an' I s'pose they could make foldin' pulpits, if there was a call."

"Land sakes, I hope there won't be!" exclaimed Mrs. Sargent. "An' the Elder never said much of anything either, though he was always preachin'! Now your husband, Mis' Baxter, always has plenty to say after you think he's all through. There's water in his well when the others is all dry!"

"But how about the pews?" interrupted Mrs. Burbank. "I think Nancy's idea is splendid, and I want to see it carried out. We might make it a picnic, bring our luncheons, and work all together; let every woman in the congregation come and scrub her own pew."

"Some are too old, others live at too great a distance," and the minister's wife sighed a little; "indeed, most of those who once owned the pews or sat in them seemed to be dead, or gone away to live in busier places."

"I've no patience with 'em, gallivantin' over the earth," and here Lobelia rose and shook the carpet threads from her lap. "I shouldn't want to live in a livelier place than Edgewood, seem's though! We wash and hang out Mondays, iron Tuesdays, cook Wednesdays, clean house and mend Thursdays and Fridays, bake Saturdays, and go to meetin' Sundays. I don't hardly see how they can do any more 'n that in Chicago!"

"Never mind if we have lost members!" said the indomitable Mrs. Burbank. "The members we still have left must work all the harder. We'll each clean our own pew, then take a few of our neighbours', and then hire Mrs. Simpson to do the wainscoting and floor. Can we scrub Friday and lay the carpet Saturday? My husband and Deacon Miller can help us at the end of the week. All in favour manifest it by the usual sign. Contrary minded? It is a vote."

There never were any contrary minded when Mrs. Jere Burbank was in the chair. Public sentiment in Edgewood was swayed by the Dorcas Society, but Mrs. Burbank swayed the Dorcases themselves as the wind sways the wheat.

CHAPTER II

T he old Meeting House wore an animated aspect when the eventful Friday came, a cold, brilliant, sparkling December day, with good sleighing, and with energy in every breath that swept over the dazzling snowfields. The sexton had built a fire in the furnace on the way to his morning work—a fire so economically contrived that it would last exactly the four or five necessary hours, and not a second more. At eleven o'clock all the pillars of the society had assembled, having finished their own household work and laid out on their respective kitchen tables comfortable luncheons for the men of the family, if they were fortunate enough to number any among their luxuries. Water was heated upon oil-stoves set about here and there, and there was a brave array of scrubbing-brushes, cloths, soap, and even sand and soda, for it had been decided and manifested-by-the-usual-sign-and-no-contrary-minded-and-it-was-a-vote that the dirt was to come off, whether the paint came with it or not. Each of the fifteen women present selected a block of seats, preferably one in which her own was situated, and all fell busily to work.

"There is nobody here to clean the right-wing pews," said Nancy Wentworth, "so I will take those for my share."

"You're not making a very wise choice, Nancy," and the minister's wife smiled as she spoke. "The infant class of the Sunday-school sits there, you know, and I expect the paint has had extra wear and tear. Families don't seem to occupy those pews regularly nowadays."

"I can remember when every seat in the whole church was filled, wings an' all," mused Mrs. Sargent, wringing out her wascloth in a reminiscent mood. "The one in front o' you, Nancy, was always called the 'deef pew' in the old times, and all the folks that was hard o' hearin' used to congregate there."

"The next pew hasn't been occupied since I came here," said the minister's wife.

"No," answered Mrs. Sargent, glad of any opportunity to retail neighbourhood news. "'Squire Bean's folks have moved to Portland to be with the married daughter. Somebody has to stay with her, and her husband won't. The 'Squire ain't a strong man, and he's most too old to go to meetin' now. The youngest son has just died in New York, so I hear."

"What ailed him?" inquired Maria Sharp.

"I guess he was completely wore out takin' care of his health," returned Mrs. Sargent. "He had a splendid constitution from a boy, but he was always afraid it wouldn't last him.—The seat back o' 'Squire Bean's is the old Peabody pew—ain't that the Peabody pew you're scrubbin', Nancy?"

"I believe so," Nancy answered, never pausing in her labours. "It's so long since anybody sat there, it's hard to remember."

"It is the Peabodys', I know it, because the aisle runs right up facin' it. I can see old Deacon Peabody settin' in this end same as if 'twas yesterday."

"He had died before Jere and I came back here to live," said Mrs. Burbank. "The first I remember, Justin Peabody sat in the end seat; the sister that died, next, and in the corner, against the wall, Mrs. Peabody, with a crêpe shawl and a palm-leaf fan. They were a handsome family. You used to sit with them sometimes, Nancy; Esther was great friends with you."

"Yes, she was," Nancy replied, lifting the tattered cushion from its place and brushing it; "and I with her.—What is the use of scrubbing and carpeting, when there are only twenty pew-cushions and six hassocks in the whole church, and most of them ragged? How can I ever mend this?"

"I shouldn't trouble myself to darn other people's cushions!"

This unchristian sentiment came in Mrs. Miller's ringing tones from the rear of the church.

"I don't know why," argued Maria Sharp. "I'm going to mend my Aunt Achsa's cushion, and we haven't spoken for years; but hers is the next pew to mine, and I'm going to have my part of the church look decent, even if she is too stingy to do her share. Besides, there aren't any Peabodys left to do their own darning, and Nancy was friends with Esther."

"Yes, it's nothing more than right," Nancy replied, with a note of relief in her voice, "considering Esther."

"Though he don't belong to the scrubbin' sex, there is one Peabody alive, as you know, if you stop to think, Maria; for Justin's alive, and livin' out West somewheres. At least, he's as much alive as ever he was; he was as good as dead when he was twenty-one, but his mother was always too soft-hearted to bury him."

There was considerable laughter over this sally of the outspoken Mrs. Sargent, whose keen wit was the delight of the neighbourhood.

"I know he's alive and doing business in Detroit, for I got his address a week or ten days ago, and wrote, asking him if he'd like to give a couple of dollars toward repairing the old church."

Everybody looked at Mrs. Burbank with interest.

"Hasn't he answered?" asked Maria Sharp.

Nancy Wentworth held her breath, turned her face to the wall, and silently wiped the paint of the wainscoting. The blood that had rushed into her cheeks at Mrs. Sargent's jeering reference to Justin Peabody still lingered there for any one who ran to read, but fortunately nobody ran; they were too busy scrubbing.

"Not yet. Folks don't hurry about answering when you ask them for a contribution," replied the president, with a cynicism common to persons who collect funds for charitable purposes. "George Wickham sent me twenty-five cents from Denver. When I wrote him a receipt, I said thank you same as Aunt Polly did when the neighbours brought her a piece of beef: 'Ever so much obleeged, but don't forget me when you come to kill a pig.'—Now, Mrs. Baxter, you shan't clean James Bruce's pew, or what was his before he turned Second Advent. I'll do that myself, for he used to be in my Sunday-school class."

"He's the backbone o' that congregation now," asserted Mrs. Sargent, "and they say he's goin' to marry Mrs. Sam Peters, who sings in their choir as soon as his year is up. They make a perfect fool of him in that church."

"You can't make a fool of a man that nature ain't begun with," argued Miss Brewster. "Jim Bruce never was very strong-minded, but I declare it seems to me that when men lose their wives, they lose their wits! I was sure Jim would marry Hannah Thompson that keeps house for him. I suspected she was lookin' out for a life job when she hired out with him."

"Hannah Thompson may keep Jim's house, but she'll never keep Jim, that's certain!" affirmed the president; "and I can't see that Mrs. Peters will better herself much."

"I don't blame her, for one!" came in no uncertain tones from the left-wing pews, and the Widow Buzzell rose from her knees and approached the group by the pulpit. "If there's anything duller than cookin' three meals a day *for* yourself, and settin' down and eatin' 'em *by* yourself, and then gettin' up and clearin' 'em away *after* yourself, I'd like to know it! I shouldn't want any good-lookin', pleasant-spoken man to offer himself to me without he expected to be snapped up, that's all! But if you've made out to get one husband in York County, you can thank the Lord and not expect any more favours. I used to think Tom was poor comp'ny and complain I couldn't have any conversation with him, but land, I could talk at him, and there's considerable comfort in that. And I could pick up after him! Now every room in my house is clean, and every closet and bureau drawer, too; I can't start drawin' in another rug, for I've got all the rugs I can step foot on. I dried so many apples last year I shan't need to cut up any this season. My jelly and preserves ain't out, and there I am; and there most of us are, in this village, without a man to take steps for and trot 'round after! There's just three husbands among the fifteen women scrubbin' here now, and the rest of us is all old maids and widders. No wonder the men-folks die, or move away like Justin Peabody; a place with such a mess o' women-folks ain't healthy to live in, whatever Lobelia Brewster may say."

CHAPTER III

J ustin Peabody had once faithfully struggled with the practical difficulties of life in Edgewood, or so he had thought, in those old days of which Nancy Wentworth was thinking as she wiped the paint of the Peabody pew. Work in the mills did not attract him; he had no capital to invest in a stock of goods for store-keeping; school-teaching offered him only a pittance; there remained then only the farm, if he were to stay at home and keep his mother company.

"Justin don't seem to take no holt of things," said the neighbours.

"Good Heavens!" It seemed to him that there were no things to take hold of! That was his first thought; later he grew to think that the trouble all lay in himself, and both thoughts bred weakness.

The farm had somehow supported the family in the old Deacon's time, but Justin seemed unable to coax a competence from the soil. He could, and did, rise early and work late; till the earth, sow crops; but he could not make the rain fall nor the sun shine at the times he needed them, and the elements, however much they might seem to favour his neighbours, seldom smiled on his enterprises. The crows liked Justin's corn better than any other in Edgewood. It had a richness peculiar to itself, a quality that appealed to the most jaded palate, so that it was really worth while to fly over a mile of intervening fields and pay it the delicate compliment of preference.

Justin could explain the attitude of caterpillars, worms, grasshoppers, and potato-bugs toward him only by assuming that he attracted them as the magnet in the toy boxes attracts the miniature fishes.

"Land of liberty! look at 'em congregate!" ejaculated Jabe Slocum, when he was called in for consultation. "Now if you'd gone in for breedin' insecks, you could be as proud as Cuffy an' exhibit 'em at the County Fair! They'd give yer prizes for size an' numbers an' speed, I guess! Why, say, they're real crowded for room—the plants ain't give 'em enough leaves to roost on! Have you tried 'Bug Death'?"

"It acts like a tonic on them," said Justin gloomily.

"Sho! you don't say so! Now mine can't abide the sight nor smell of it. What 'bout Paris green?"

"They thrive on it; it's as good as an appetizer."

"Well," said Jabe Slocum, revolving the quid of tobacco in his mouth reflectively, "the bug that ain't got no objection to p'ison is a bug that's got ways o' thinkin' an' feelin' an' reasonin' that I ain't able to cope with! P'r'aps it's all a leadin' o' Providence. Mebbe it shows you'd ought to quit farmin' crops an' take to raisin' live stock!"

Justin did just that, as a matter of fact, a year or two later; but stock that has within itself the power of being "live" has also rare qualifications for being dead when occasion suits, and it generally did suit Justin's stock. It proved prone not only to all the general diseases that cattle-flesh is heir to, but was capable even of suicide. At least, it is true that two valuable Jersey calves, tied to stakes on the hillside, had flung themselves violently down the bank and strangled themselves with their own ropes in a manner which seemed to show that they found no pleasure in existence, at all events on the Peabody farm.

These were some of the little tragedies that had sickened young Justin Peabody with life in Edgewood, and Nancy Wentworth, even then, realized some of them and sympathized without speaking, in a girl's poor, helpless way.

Mrs. Simpson had washed the floor in the right wing of the church and Nancy had cleaned all the paint. Now she sat in the old Peabody pew darning the forlorn, faded cushion with grey carpet-thread: thread as grey as her own life.

The scrubbing-party had moved to its labours in a far corner of the church, and two of the women were beginning preparations for the basket luncheons. Nancy's needle was no busier than her memory. Long years ago she had often sat in the Peabody pew, sometimes at first as a girl of sixteen when asked by Esther, and then, on coming home from school at eighteen, "finished," she had been invited now and again by Mrs. Peabody herself, on those Sundays when her own invalid mother had not attended service.

Those were wonderful Sundays—Sundays of quiet, trembling peace and maiden joy.

Justin sat beside her, and she had been sure then, but had long since grown to doubt the evidence of her senses, that he, too, vibrated with pleasure at the nearness. Was there not a summer morning when his hand touched her white lace mitt as they held the hymn-book together, and the lines of the

Rise, my soul, and stretch thy wings,
Thy better portion trace,

became blurred on the page and melted into something indistinguishable for a full minute or two afterward? Were there not looks, and looks, and looks? Or had she some misleading trick of vision in those days? Justin's dark, handsome profile rose before her: the level brows and fine lashes; the well-cut nose and lovable mouth—the Peabody mouth and chin, somewhat too sweet and pliant for strength, perhaps. Then the eyes turned to hers in the old way, just for a fleeting glance, as they had so often done at prayer-meeting, or sociable, or Sunday service. Was it not a man's heart she had seen in them? And oh, if she could only be sure that her own woman's heart had not looked out from hers, drawn from its maiden shelter in spite of all her wish to keep it hidden!

Then followed two dreary years of indecision and suspense, when Justin's eyes met hers less freely; when his looks were always gloomy and anxious; when affairs at the Peabody farm grew worse and worse; when his mother followed her husband, the old Deacon, and her daughter Esther to the burying-ground in the churchyard. Then the end of all things came, the end of the world for Nancy: Justin's departure for the West in a very frenzy of discouragement over the narrowness and limitation and injustice of his lot; over the rockiness and barrenness and unkindness of the New England soil; over the general bitterness of fate and the "bludgeonings of chance."

He was a failure, born of a family of failures. If the world owed him a living, he had yet to find the method by which it could be earned. All this he thought and uttered, and much more of the same sort. In these days of humbled pride self was paramount, though it was a self he despised. There was no time for love. Who was he for a girl to lean upon?—he who could not stand erect himself!

He bade a stiff good-bye to his neighbours, and to Nancy he vouchsafed little more. A handshake, with no thrill of love in it such as might have furnished her palm, at least, some memories to dwell upon; a few stilted words of leave-taking; a halting, meaningless sentence or two about his "botch" of life—then he walked away from the Wentworth doorstep. But half way down the garden path, where the shrivelled hollyhocks stood like sentinels, did a wave of something different sweep over him—a wave of the boyish, irresponsible past when his heart had wings and could fly without fear to its mate—a wave of the past that was rushing through Nancy's mind, well-nigh burying her in its bitter-sweet waters! For he lifted his head, and suddenly retracing his steps, he came toward her, and, taking her hand again, said forlornly: "You'll see me back when my luck turns, Nancy."

Nancy knew that the words might mean little or much, according to the manner in which they were uttered, but to her hurt pride and sore, shamed woman-instinct, they were a promise, simply because there was a choking sound in Justin's voice and tears in Justin's eyes. "You'll see me back when my luck turns, Nancy;" this was the phrase upon which she had lived for more than ten years. Nancy had once heard the old parson say, ages ago, that the whole purpose of life was the growth of the soul; that we eat, sleep, clothe ourselves, work, love, all to give the soul another day, month, year, in which to develop. She used to wonder if her soul could be growing in the monotonous round of her dull duties and her duller pleasures. She did not confess it even to herself; nevertheless she knew that she worked, ate, slept, to live until Justin's luck turned. Her love had lain in her heart a bird without a song, year after year. Her mother had dwelt by her side and never guessed; her father too; and both were dead. The neighbours also, lynx-eyed and curious, had never suspected. If she had suffered, no one in Edgewood was any the wiser, for the maiden heart is not commonly worn on the sleeve in New England. If she had been openly pledged to Justin Peabody, she could have waited twice ten years with a decent show of self-respect, for long engagements were viewed rather as a matter of course in that neighbourhood. The endless months had gone on since that grey November day when Justin had said good-bye. It had been just before Thanksgiving, and she went to church with an aching and ungrateful heart. The parson read from the eighth chapter of St. Matthew, a most unexpected selection for that holiday. "If you can't find anything else to be thankful for," he cried, "go home and be thankful you are not a leper!"

Nancy took the drastic counsel away from the church with her, and it was many a year before she could manage to add to this slender store anything to increase her gratitude for mercies given, though all the time she was outwardly busy, cheerful, and helpful.

Justin had once come back to Edgewood, and it was the bitterest drop in her cup of bitterness that she was spending that winter in Berwick (where, so the neighbours told him, she was a great favourite in society, and was receiving much attention from gentlemen), so that she had never heard of his visit until the spring had come again. Parted friends did not keep up with one another's affairs by means of epistolary communication, in those days, in Edgewood; it was not the custom. Spoken words were difficult enough to Justin Peabody, and written words were quite impossible, especially if they were to be used to define his half-conscious desires and his fluctuations of will, or to recount his disappointments and discouragements and mistakes.

CHAPTER IV

It was Saturday afternoon, the twenty-fourth of December, and the weary sisters of the Dorcas band rose from their bruised knees and removed their little stores of carpet-tacks from their mouths. This was a feminine custom of long standing, and as no village dressmaker had ever died of pins in the digestive organs, so were no symptoms of carpet-tacks ever discovered in any Dorcas, living or dead. Men wondered at the habit and reviled it, but stood confounded in the presence of its indubitable harmlessness.

The red ingrain carpet was indeed very warm, beautiful, and comforting to the eye, and the sisters were suitably grateful to Providence, and devoutly thankful to themselves, that they had been enabled to buy, sew, and lay so many yards of it. But as they stood looking at their completed task, it was cruelly true that there was much left to do.

The aisles had been painted dark brown on each side of the red strips leading from the doors to the pulpit, but the rest of the church floor was "a thing of shreds and patches." Each member of the carpet committee had paid (as a matter of pride, however ill she could afford it) three dollars and sixty-seven cents for sufficient carpet to lay in her own pew; but these brilliant spots of conscientious effort only made the stretches of bare, unpainted floor more evident. And that was not all. Traces of former spasmodic and individual efforts desecrated the present ideals. The doctor's pew had a pink and blue Brussels on it; the lawyer's, striped stair-carpeting; the Browns from Deerwander sported straw matting and were not abashed; while the Greens, the Whites, the Blacks and the Greys displayed floor coverings as dissimilar as their names.

"I never noticed it before!" exclaimed Maria Sharp, "but it ain't Christian, that floor! it's heathenish and ungodly!"

"For mercy's sake, don't swear, Maria," said Mrs. Miller nervously. "We've done our best, and let's hope that folks will look up and not down. It isn't as if they were going to set in the chandelier; they'll have something else to think about when Nancy gets her hemlock branches and white carnations in the pulpit vases. This morning my Abner picked off two pinks from the plant I've been nursing in my dining-room for weeks, trying to make it bloom for Christmas. I slapped his hands good, and it's been haunting me ever since to think I had to correct him the day before Christmas—Come, Lobelia, we must be hurrying!"

"One thing comforts me," exclaimed the Widow Buzzell, as she took her hammer and tacks preparatory to leaving; "and that is that the Methodist meetin'-house ain't got any carpet at all."

"Mrs. Buzzell, Mrs. Buzzell!" interrupted the minister's wife, with a smile that took the sting from her speech. "It will be like punishing little Abner Miller; if we think those thoughts on Christmas Eve, we shall surely be haunted afterward."

"And anyway," interjected Maria Sharp, who always saved the situation, "you just wait and see if the Methodists don't say they'd rather have no carpet at all than have one that don't go all over the floor. I know 'em!" and she put on her hood and blanket-shawl as she gave one last fond look at the improvements.

"I'm going home to get my supper, and come back afterward to lay the carpet in my pew; my beans and brown bread will be just right by now, and perhaps it will rest me a little; besides, I must feed 'Zekiel."

As Nancy Wentworth spoke, she sat in a corner of her own modest rear seat, looking a little pale and tired. Her waving dark hair had loosened and fallen over her cheeks, and her eyes gleamed from under it wistfully. Nowadays Nancy's eyes never had the sparkle of gazing into the future, but always the liquid softness that comes from looking backward.

"The church will be real cold by then, Nancy," objected Mrs. Burbank.—"Good-night, Mrs. Baxter."

"Oh, no! I shall be back by half-past six, and I shall not work long. Do you know what I believe I'll do, Mrs. Burbank, just through the holidays? Christmas and New Year's both coming on Sunday this year, there'll be a great many out to church, not counting the strangers that'll come to the special service to-morrow. Instead of putting down my own pew carpet that'll never be noticed here in the back, I'll lay it in the old Peabody pew, for the red aisle-strip leads straight up to it; the ministers always go up that side, and it does look forlorn."

"That's so! And all the more because my pew, that's exactly opposite in the left wing, is new carpeted and cushioned," replied the president. "I think it's real generous of you, Nancy, because the Riverboro folks, knowing that you're a member of the carpet committee, will be sure to notice, and think it's queer you haven't made an effort to carpet your own pew."

"Never mind!" smiled Nancy wearily. "Riverboro folks never go to bed on Saturday nights without wondering what Edgewood is thinking about them!"

The minister's wife stood at her window watching Nancy as she passed the parsonage.

"How wasted! How wasted!" she sighed. "Going home to eat her lonely supper and feed 'Zekiel . . . I can bear it for the others, but not for Nancy . . . Now she has lighted her lamp, now she has put fresh pine on the fire, for new smoke comes from the chimney. Why should I sit down and serve my dear husband, and Nancy feed 'Zekiel?"

There was some truth in Mrs. Baxter's feeling. Mrs. Buzzell, for instance, had three sons; Maria Sharp was absorbed in her lame father and her Sunday-school work; and Lobelia Brewster would not have considered matrimony a blessing, even under the most favourable conditions. But Nancy was framed and planned for other things, and 'Zekiel was an insufficient channel for her soft, womanly sympathy and her bright activity of mind and body.

'Zekiel had lost his tail in a mowing-machine; 'Zekiel had the asthma, and the immersion of his nose in milk made him sneeze, so he was wont to slip his paw in and out of the dish and lick it patiently for five minutes together. Nancy often watched him pityingly, giving him kind and gentle words to sustain his fainting spirit, but to-night she paid no heed to him, although he sneezed violently to attract her attention.

She had put her supper on the lighted table by the kitchen window and was pouring out her cup of tea, when a boy rapped at the door. "Here's a paper and a letter, Miss Wentworth," he said. "It's the second this week, and they think over to the store that that Berwick widower must be settin' up and takin' notice!"

She had indeed received a letter the day before, an unsigned communication, consisting only of the words, "Second Epistle of John. Verse 12."

She had taken her Bible to look out the reference and found it to be:—

"Having many things to write unto you, I would not write with paper and ink; but I trust to come unto you, and speak face to face, that our joy may be full."

The envelope was postmarked New York, and she smiled, thinking that Mrs. Emerson, a charming lady who had spent the summer in Edgewood, and had sung with her in the village choir, was coming back, as she had promised, to have a sleigh ride and see Edgewood in its winter dress. Nancy had almost forgotten the first letter in the excitements of her busy day, and now here was another, from Boston this time. She opened the envelope and found again only a single sentence, printed, not written. (Lest she should guess the hand, she wondered?)

"Second Epistle of John. Verse 5."

"And now I beseech thee, lady, not as though I wrote a new commandment unto thee, but that which we had from the beginning, that we love one another."

Was it Mrs. Emerson? Could it be—any one else? Was it—? No, it might have been, years ago; but not now; not now!—And yet; he was always so different from other people; and once, in church, he had handed her the hymn-book with his finger pointing to a certain verse.

She always fancied that her secret fidelity of heart rose from the fact that Justin Peabody was "different." From the hour of their first acquaintance, she was ever comparing him with his companions, and always to his advantage. So long as a woman finds all men very much alike (as Lobelia Brewster did, save that she allowed some to be worse!), she is in no danger. But the moment in which she perceives and discriminates subtle differences, marvelling that there can be two opinions about a man's superiority, that moment the miracle has happened.

"And now I beseech thee, lady, not as though I wrote a new commandment unto thee, but that which we had from the beginning, that we love one another."

No, it could not be from Justin. She drank her tea, played with her beans abstractedly, and nibbled her slice of steaming brown bread.

"Not as though I wrote a new commandment unto thee."

No, not a new one; twelve, fifteen years old, that commandment!

"That we love one another."

Who was speaking? Who had written these words? The first letter sounded just like Mrs. Emerson, who had said she was a very poor correspondent, but that she should just "drop down" on Nancy one of these days; but this second letter never came from Mrs. Emerson.—Well, there would be an explanation some time; a pleasant one; one to smile over, and tell 'Zekiel and repeat to the neighbours; but not an unexpected, sacred, beautiful explanation, such a one as the heart of a woman could imagine, if she were young enough and happy enough to hope.

She washed her cup and plate; replaced the uneaten beans in the brown pot, and put them away with the round loaf, folded the cloth (Lobelia Brewster said Nancy always "set out her meals as if she was entertainin' company from Portland"), closed the stove dampers, carried the lighted lamp to a safe corner shelf, and lifted 'Zekiel to his cushion on the high-backed rocker, doing all with the nice precision of long habit. Then she wrapped herself warmly, and locking the lonely little house behind her, set out to finish her work in the church.

CHAPTER V

A t this precise moment Justin Peabody was eating his own beans and brown bread (articles of diet of which his Detroit landlady was lamentably ignorant) at the new tavern, not far from the meeting-house.

It would not be fair to him to say that Mrs. Burbank's letter had brought him back to Edgewood, but it had certainly accelerated his steps.

For the first six years after Justin Peabody left home, he had drifted about from place to place, saving every possible dollar of his uncertain earnings in the conscious hope that he could go back to New England and ask Nancy Wentworth to marry him. The West was prosperous and progressive, but how he yearned, in idle moments, for the grimmer and more sterile soil that had given him birth!

Then came what seemed to him a brilliant chance for a lucky turn of his savings, and he invested them in an enterprise which, wonderfully as it promised, failed within six months and left him penniless. At that moment he definitely gave up all hope, and for the next few years he put Nancy as far as possible out of his mind, in the full belief that he was acting an honourable part in refusing to drag her into his tangled and fruitless way of life. If she ever did care for him,—and he could not be sure, she was always so shy,—she must have outgrown the feeling long since, and be living happily, or at least contentedly, in her own way. He was glad in spite of himself when he heard that she had never married; but at least he hadn't it on his conscience that *he* had kept her single!

On the seventeenth of December, Justin, his business day over, was walking toward the dreary house in which he ate and slept. As he turned the corner, he heard one woman say to another, as they watched a man stumbling sorrowfully down the street: "Going home will be the worst of all for him—to find nobody there!" That was what going home had meant for him these ten years, but he afterward felt it strange that this thought should have struck him so forcibly on that particular day. Entering the boarding-house, he found Mrs. Burbank's letter with its Edgewood postmark on the hall table, and took it up to his room. He kindled a little fire in the air-tight stove, watching the flame creep from shavings to kindlings, from kindlings to small pine, and from small pine to the round, hardwood sticks; then when the result seemed certain, he closed the stove door and sat down to read the letter. Whereupon all manner of strange things happened in his head and heart and flesh and spirit as he sat there alone, his hands in his pockets, his feet braced against the legs of the stove.

It was a cold winter night, and the snow and sleet beat against the windows. He looked about the ugly room: at the washstand with its square of oilcloth in front and its detestable bowl and pitcher; at the rigours of his white iron bedstead, with the valley in the middle of the lumpy mattress and the darns in the rumpled pillowcases; at the dull photographs of the landlady's hideous husband and children enshrined on the mantelshelf; looked at the abomination of desolation surrounding him until his soul sickened and cried out like a child's for something more like home. It was as if a spring thaw had melted his ice-bound heart, and on the crest of a wave it was drifting out into the milder waters of some unknown sea. He could have laid his head in the kind lap of a woman and cried: "Comfort me! Give me companionship or I die!"

The wind howled in the chimney and rattled the loose window-sashes; the snow, freezing as it fell, dashed against the glass with hard, cutting little blows; at least, that is the way in which the wind and snow flattered themselves they were making existence disagreeable to Justin Peabody when he read the letter; but never were elements more mistaken.

It was a June Sunday in the boarding-house bedroom; and for that matter it was not the boarding-house bedroom at all: it was the old Orthodox church on Tory Hill in Edgewood.

The windows were wide open, and the smell of the purple clover and the humming of the bees were drifting into the sweet, wide spaces within. Justin was sitting in the end of the Peabody pew, and Nancy Wentworth was beside him; Nancy, cool and restful in her white dress; dark-haired Nancy under the shadow of her shirred muslin hat.

Rise, my soul, and stretch thy wings,
Thy better portion trace.

The melodeon gave the tune, and Nancy and he stood to sing, taking the book between them. His hand touched hers, and as the music of the hymn rose and fell, the future unrolled itself before his eyes; a future in which Nancy was his wedded wife; and the happy years stretched on and on in front of them until there was a row of little heads in the old Peabody pew, and mother and father could look proudly along the line at the young things they were bringing into the house of the Lord.

The recalling of that vision worked like magic in Justin's blood. His soul rose and stretched its wings and "traced its better portion" vividly, as he sprang to his feet and walked up and down the bedroom floor. He would get a few days' leave and go back to Edgewood for Christmas, to join, with all the old neighbours, in the service at the meeting-house; and in pursuance of this resolve, he shook his fist in the face of the landlady's husband on the mantelpiece and dared him to prevent.

He had a salary of fifty dollars a month, with some very slight prospect of an increase after January. He did not see how two persons could eat, and drink, and lodge, and dress on it in Detroit, but he proposed to give Nancy Wentworth the refusal of that magnificent future, that brilliant and tempting offer. He had exactly one hundred dollars in the bank, and sixty or seventy of them would be spent in the journeys, counting two happy, blessed fares back from Edgewood to Detroit; and if he paid only his own fare back, he would throw the price of the other into the pond behind the Wentworth house. He would drop another ten dollars into the plate on Christmas Day toward the repairs on the church; if he starved, he would do that. He was a failure. Everything his hand touched turned to naught. He looked himself full in the face, recognizing his weakness, and in this supremest moment of recognition he was a stronger man than he had been an hour before. His drooping shoulders had straightened; the restless look had gone from his eyes; his sombre face had something of repose in it, the repose of a settled purpose. He was a failure, but perhaps if he took the risks (and if Nancy would take them—but that was the trouble, women were so unselfish, they were always willing to take risks, and one ought not to let them!), perhaps he might do better in trying to make a living for two than he had in working for himself alone. He would go home, tell Nancy that he was an unlucky good-for-naught, and ask her if she would try her hand at making him over.

CHAPTER VI

These were the reasons that had brought Justin Peabody to Edgewood on the Saturday afternoon before Christmas, and had taken him to the new tavern on Tory Hill, near the Meeting-House.

Nobody recognized him at the station or noticed him at the tavern, and after his supper he put on his overcoat and started out for a walk, aimlessly hoping that he might meet a friend, or failing that, intending to call on some of his old neighbours, with the view of hearing the village news and securing some information which might help him to decide when he had better lay himself and his misfortunes at Nancy Wentworth's feet. They were pretty feet! He remembered that fact well enough under the magical influence of familiar sights and sounds and odours. He was restless, miserable, anxious, homesick—not for Detroit, but for some heretofore unimagined good; yet, like Bunyan's shepherd boy in the Valley of Humiliation, he carried "the herb called Hearts-ease in his bosom," for he was at last loving consciously.

How white the old church looked, and how green the blinds! It must have been painted very lately: that meant that the parish was fairly prosperous. There were new shutters in the belfry tower, too; he remembered the former open space and the rusty bell, and he liked the change. Did the chimney use to be in that corner? No; but his father had always said it would have drawn better if it had been put there in the beginning. New shingles within a year: that was evident to a practised eye. He wondered if anything had been done to the inside of the building, but he must wait until the morrow to see, for, of course, the doors would be locked. No; the one at the right side was ajar. He opened it softly and stepped into the tiny square entry that he recalled so well—the one through which the Sunday-school children ran out to the steps from their catechism, apparently enjoying the sunshine after a spell of orthodoxy; the little entry where the village girls congregated while waiting for the last bell to ring—they made a soft blur of pink and blue and buff, a little flutter of curls and braids and fans and sunshades, in his mind's eye, as he closed the outer door behind him and gently opened the inner one. The church was flooded with moonlight and snowlight, and there was one lamp burning at the back of the pulpit; a candle, too, on the pulpit steps. There was the tip-tap-tip of a tack-hammer going on in a distant corner. Was somebody hanging Christmas garlands? The new red carpet attracted his notice, and as he grew accustomed to the dim light, it carried his eye along the aisle he had trod so many years of Sundays, to the old familiar pew. The sound of the hammer ceased and a woman rose from her knees. A stranger was doing for the family honour what he ought himself to have done. The woman turned to shake her skirt, and it was Nancy Wentworth. He might have known it. Women were always faithful; they always remembered old landmarks, old days, old friends, old duties. His father and mother and Esther were all gone; who but dear Nancy would have made the old Peabody pew right and tidy for the Christmas festival? Bless her kind womanly heart!

She looked just the same to him as when he last saw her. Mercifully he seemed to have held in remembrance all these years not so much her youthful bloom as her general qualities of mind and heart: her cheeriness, her spirit, her unflagging zeal, her bright womanliness. Her grey dress was turned up in front over a crimson moreen petticoat. She had on a cosy jacket, a fur turban of some sort with a redbreast in it, and her cheeks were flushed from exertion. "Sweet records, and promises as sweet," had always met in Nancy's face, and either he had forgotten how pretty she was, or else she had absolutely grown prettier during his absence.

Nancy would have chosen the supreme moment of meeting very differently, but she might well have chosen worse. She unpinned her skirt and brushed the threads off, smoothed the pew cushions carefully, and took a last stitch in the ragged hassock. She then lifted the Bible and the hymn-book from the rack, and putting down a bit of flannel on the pulpit steps, took a flatiron from an oil-stove, and opening the ancient books, pressed out the well-thumbed leaves one by one with infinite care. After replacing the volumes in their accustomed place, she first extinguished the flame of her stove, which she tucked out of sight, and then blew out the lamp and the candle. The church was still light enough for objects to be seen in a shadowy way, like the objects in a dream, and Justin did not realize that he was a man in the flesh, looking at a woman; spying, it might

The Old Peabody Pew : A Christmas Romance of a Country Church

be, upon her privacy. He was one part of a dream and she another, and he stood as if waiting, and fearing, to be awakened.

Nancy, having done all, came out of the pew, and standing in the aisle, looked back at the scene of her labours with pride and content. And as she looked, some desire to stay a little longer in the dear old place must have come over her, or some dread of going back to her lonely cottage, for she sat down in Justin's corner of the pew with folded hands, her eyes fixed dreamily on the pulpit and her ears hearing: "Not as though I wrote a new commandment unto thee, but that which we had from the beginning."

Justin's grasp on the latch tightened as he prepared to close the door and leave the place, but his instinct did not warn him quickly enough, after all, for, obeying some uncontrollable impulse, Nancy suddenly fell on her knees in the pew and buried her face in the cushions.

The dream broke, and in an instant Justin was a man—worse than that, he was an eavesdropper, ashamed of his unsuspected presence. He felt himself standing, with covered head and feet shod, in the holy temple of a woman's heart.

But his involuntary irreverence brought abundant grace with it. The glimpse and the revelation wrought their miracles silently and irresistibly, not by the slow processes of growth which Nature demands for her enterprises, but with the sudden swiftness of the spirit. In an instant changes had taken place in Justin's soul which his so-called "experiencing religion" twenty-five years back had been powerless to effect. He had indeed been baptized then, but the recording angel could have borne witness that this second baptism fructified the first, and became the real herald of the new birth and the new creature.

CHAPTER VII

Justin Peabody silently closed the inner door, and stood in the entry with his head bent and his heart in a whirl until he should hear Nancy rise to her feet. He must take this Heaven-sent chance of telling her all, but how do it without alarming her?

A moment, and her step sounded in the stillness of the empty church.

Obeying the first impulse, he passed through the outer door, and standing on the step, knocked once, twice, three times; then, opening it a little and speaking through the chink, he called, "Is Miss Nancy Wentworth here?"

"I'm here!" in a moment came Nancy's answer, and then, with a little wondering tremor in her voice, as if a hint of the truth had already dawned: "What's wanted?"

"You're wanted, Nancy, wanted badly, by Justin Peabody, come back from the West."

The door opened wide, and Justin faced Nancy standing half-way down the aisle, her eyes brilliant, her lips parted. A week ago Justin's apparition confronting her in the empty Meeting-House after nightfall, even had she been prepared for it as now, by his voice, would have terrified her beyond measure. Now it seemed almost natural and inevitable. She had spent these last days in the church where both of them had been young and happy together; the two letters had brought him vividly to mind, and her labour in the old Peabody pew had been one long excursion into the past in which he was the most prominent and the best-loved figure.

"I said I'd come back to you when my luck turned, Nancy."

These were so precisely the words she expected him to say, should she ever see him again face to face, that for an additional moment they but heightened her sense of unreality.

"Well, the luck hasn't turned, after all, but I couldn't wait any longer. Have you given a thought to me all these years, Nancy?"

"More than one, Justin"; for the very look upon his face, the tenderness of his voice, the attitude of his body, outran his words and told her what he had come home to say, told her that her years of waiting were over at last.

"You ought to despise me for coming back again with only myself and my empty hands to offer you."

How easy it was to speak his heart out in this dim and quiet place! How tongue-tied he would have been, sitting on the black haircloth sofa in the Wentworth parlour and gazing at the open soapstone stove!

"Oh, men are such fools!" cried Nancy, smiles and tears struggling together in her speech, as she sat down suddenly in her own pew and put her hands over her face.

"They are," agreed Justin humbly, "but I've never stopped loving you, whenever I've had time for thinking or loving. And I wasn't sure that you really cared anything about me; and how could I have asked you when I hadn't a dollar in the world?"

"There are other things to give a woman besides dollars, Justin."

"Are there? Well, you shall have them all, every one of them, Nancy, if you can make up your mind to do without the dollars; for dollars seem to be just what I can't manage."

Her hand was in his by this time, and they were sitting side by side in the cushionless, carpetless Wentworth pew. The door stood open; the winter moon shone in upon them. That it was beginning to grow cold in the church passed unnoticed. The grasp of the woman's hand seemed to give the man new hope and courage, and Justin's warm, confiding, pleading pressure brought balm to Nancy, balm and healing for the wounds her pride had suffered; joy, too, half-conscious still, that her life need not be lived to the end in unfruitful solitude. She had waited, "as some grey lake lies, full and smooth, awaiting the star below the twilight." Justin Peabody might have been no other woman's star, but he was Nancy's!

"Just you sitting beside me here makes me feel as if I'd been asleep or dead all these years, and just born over again," said Justin. "I've led a respectable, hard-working, honest life, Nancy," he continued, "and I don't owe any man a cent; the trouble is that no man owes me one. I've got enough money to pay two fares back to Detroit on Monday, although I was terribly afraid you wouldn't let me do it. It'll need a good deal of thinking and planning, Nancy, for we shall be very poor."

Nancy had been storing up fidelity and affection deep, deep in the hive of her heart all these years, and now the honey of her helpfulness stood ready to be gathered.

"Could I keep hens in Detroit?" she asked. "I can always make them pay."

"Hens—in three rooms, Nancy?"

Her face fell. "And no yard?"

"No yard."

A moment's pause, and then the smile came. "Oh, well, I've had yards and hens for thirty-five years. Doing without them will be a change. I can take in sewing."

"No, you can't, Nancy. I need your backbone and wits and pluck and ingenuity, but if I can't ask you to sit with your hands folded for the rest of your life, as I'd like to, you shan't use them for other people. You're marrying me to make a man of me, but I'm not marrying you to make you a drudge."

His voice rang clear and true in the silence, and Nancy's heart vibrated at the sound.

"Oh, Justin, Justin!" she whispered. "There's something wrong somewhere, but we'll find it out together, you and I, and make it right. You're not like a failure. You don't even *look* poor, Justin; there isn't a man in Edgewood to compare with you, or I should be washing his dishes and darning his stockings this minute. And I am not a pauper! There'll be the rent of my little house and a carload of my furniture, so you can put the three-room idea out of your mind, and your firm will offer you a larger salary when you tell them you have a wife to take care of. Oh, I see it all, and it is as easy and bright and happy as can be!"

Justin put his arm around her and drew her close, with such a throb of gratitude for her belief and trust that it moved him almost to tears.

There was a long pause: then he said:—

"Now I shall call for you to-morrow morning after the last bell has stopped ringing, and we will walk up the aisle together and sit in the old Peabody pew. We shall be a nine-days' wonder anyway, but this will be equal to an announcement, especially if you take my arm. We don't either of us like to be stared at, but this will show without a word what we think

The Old Peabody Pew : A Christmas Romance of a Country Church

of each other and what we've promised to be to each other, and it's the only thing that will make me feel sure of you and settled in my mind after all these mistaken years. Have you got the courage, Nancy?"

"I shouldn't wonder! I guess if I've had courage enough to wait for you, I've got courage enough to walk up the aisle with you and marry you besides!" said Nancy.—"Now it is too late for us to stay here any longer, and you must see me only as far as my gate, for perhaps you haven't forgotten yet how interested the Brewsters are in their neighbours."

They stood at the little Wentworth gate for a moment, hand close clasped in hand. The night was clear, the air was cold and sparkling, but with nothing of bitterness in it; the sky was steely blue and the evening star glowed and burned like a tiny sun. Nancy remembered the shepherd's song she had taught the Sunday-school children, and repeated softly:—

For I my sheep was watching
Beneath the silent skies,
When sudden, far to eastward,
I saw a star arise;
Then all the peaceful heavens
With sweetest music rang,
And glory, glory, glory!
The happy angels sang.

So I this night am joyful,
Though I can scarce tell why,
It seemeth me that glory
Hath met us very nigh;
And we, though poor and humble,
Have part in heavenly plan,
For, born to-night, the Prince of Peace
Shall rule the heart of man.

Justin's heart melted within him like wax to the woman's vision and the woman's touch.

"Oh, Nancy, Nancy!" he whispered. "If I had brought my bad luck to you long, long ago, would you have taken me then, and have I lost years of such happiness as this?"

"There are some things it is not best for a man to be certain about," said Nancy, with a wise smile and a last good-night.

CHAPTER VIII

"Ring out, sweet bells,
O'er woods and dells
Your lovely strains repeat,
While happy throngs
With joyous songs
Each accent gladly greet."

Christmas morning in the old Tory Hill Meeting-House was felt by all of the persons who were present in that particular year to be a most exciting and memorable occasion.

The old sexton quite outdid himself, for although he had rung the bell for more than thirty years, he had never felt greater pride or joy in his task. Was not his son John home for Christmas, and John's wife, and a grandchild newly named Nathaniel for himself? Were there not spareribs and turkeys and cranberries and mince pies on the pantry shelves, and barrels of rosy Baldwins in the cellar and bottles of mother's root beer just waiting to give a holiday pop? The bell itself forgot its age and the suspicion of a crack that dulled its voice on a damp day, and, inspired by the bright, frosty air, the sexton's inspiring pull, and the Christmas spirit, gave out nothing but joyous tones.

Ding-dong! Ding-dong! It fired the ambitions of star scholars about to recite hymns and sing solos. It thrilled little girls expecting dolls before night. It excited beyond bearing dozens of little boys being buttoned into refractory overcoats. Ding-dong! Ding-dong! Mothers' fingers trembled when they heard it, and mothers' voices cried: "If that is the second bell, the children will never be ready in time! Where are the overshoes? Where are the mittens? Hurry, Jack! Hurry, Jennie!" Ding-dong! Ding-dong! "Where's Sally's muff? Where's father's fur cap? Is the sleigh at the door? Are the hot soapstones in? Have all of you your money for the contribution box?"

The Old Peabody Pew : A Christmas Romance of a Country Church

Ding-dong! Ding-dong! It was a blithe bell, a sweet, true bell, a holy bell, and to Justin, pacing his tavern room, as to Nancy, trembling in her maiden chamber, it rang a Christmas message:—

Awake, glad heart! Arise and sing;
It is the birthday of thy King!

The congregation filled every seat in the old Meeting-House.

As Maria Sharp had prophesied, there was one ill-natured spinster from a rival village who declared that the church floor looked like Joseph's coat laid out smooth; but in the general chorus of admiration, approval, and good will, this envious speech, though repeated from mouth to mouth, left no sting.

Another item of interest long recalled was the fact that on that august and unapproachable day the pulpit vases stood erect and empty, though Nancy Wentworth had filled them every Sunday since any one could remember. This instance, though felt at the time to be of mysterious significance if the cause were ever revealed, paled into nothingness when, after the ringing of the last bell, Nancy Wentworth walked up the aisle on Justin Peabody's arm, and they took their seats side by side in the old family pew.

("And consid'able close, too, though there was plenty o' room!")

("And no one that I ever heard of so much as suspicioned that they had ever kept company!")

("And do you s'pose she knew Justin was expected back when she scrubbed his pew a-Friday?")

("And this explains the empty pulpit vases!")

("And I always said that Nancy would make a real handsome couple if she ever got anybody to couple with!")

During the unexpected and solemn procession of the two up the aisle the soprano of the village choir stopped short in the middle of the Doxology, and the three other voices carried it to the end without any treble. Also, among those present there were some who could not remember afterward the precise petitions wafted upward in the opening prayer.

And could it be explained otherwise than by cheerfully acknowledging the bounty of an overruling Providence that Nancy Wentworth should have had a new winter dress for the first time in five years—a winter dress of dark brown cloth to match her beaver muff and victorine? The existence of this toilette had been known and discussed in Edgewood for a month past, and it was thought to be nothing more than a proper token of respect from a member of the carpet committee to the general magnificence of the church on the occasion of its reopening after repairs. Indeed, you could have identified every member of the Dorcas Society that Sunday morning by the freshness of her apparel. The brown dress, then, was generally expected; but why the white cashmere waist with collar and cuffs of point lace, devised only and suitable only for the minister's wedding, where it first saw the light?

"The white waist can only be explained as showing distinct hope!" whispered the minister's wife during the reading of the church notices.

"To me it shows more than hope; I am very sure that Nancy would never take any wear out of that lace for hope; it means certainty!" answered Maria, who was always strong in the prophetic line.

By sermon time Justin's identity had dawned upon most of the congregation. A stranger to all but one or two at first, his presence in the Peabody pew brought his face and figure back, little by little, to the minds of the old parishioners.

When the contribution plate was passed, the sexton always began at the right-wing pews, as all the sextons before him had done for a hundred years. Every eye in the church was already turned upon Justin and Nancy, and it was with almost a gasp that those in the vicinity saw a ten dollar bill fall in the plate. The sexton reeled, or, if that is too intemperate a word for a pillar of the church, the good man tottered, but caught hold of the pew rail with one hand, and, putting the thumb of his other over the bill, proceeded quickly to the next pew, lest the stranger should think better of his gift, or demand change, as had occasionally been done in the olden time.

Nancy never fluttered an eyelash, but sat quietly by Justin's side with her bosom rising and falling under the beaver fur and her cold hands clasped tight in the little brown muff. Far from grudging this appreciable part of their slender resources, she thrilled with pride to see Justin's offering fall in the plate.

Justin was too absorbed in his own thoughts to notice anything, but his munificent contribution had a most unexpected effect upon his reputation, after all; for on that day, and on many another later one, when his sudden marriage and departure with Nancy Wentworth were under discussion, the neighbours said to one another:—

"Justin must be making money fast out West! He put ten dollars in the contribution plate a-Sunday, and paid the minister ten more next day for marryin' him to Nancy; so the Peabody luck has turned at last!" which, as a matter of fact, it had.

"And all the time," said the chairman of the carpet committee to the treasurer of the Dorcas Society—"all the time, little as she realized it, Nancy was laying the carpet in her own pew. Now she's married to Justin she'll be the makin' of him, or I miss my guess. You can't do a thing with men folks without they're right alongside where you can keep your eye and hand on 'em. Justin's handsome and good and stiddy; all he need is some nice woman to put starch into him. The Edgewood Peabodys never had a mite o' stiffenin' in 'em,—limp as dishrags, every blessed one! Nancy Wentworth fairly rustles with starch. Justin hadn't been engaged to her but a few hours when they walked up the aisle together, but did you notice the way he carried his head? I declare I thought 't would fall off behind! I shouldn't wonder a mite but they prospered and come back every summer to set in the old Peabody Pew."